Franklin and the Contest

From an episode of the animated TV series *Franklin*, produced by Nelvana Limited, Neurones France s.a.r.l. and Neurones Luxembourg S.A., based on the Franklin books by Paulette Bourgeois and Brenda Clark.

Story written by Sharon Jennings.

Illustrated by Sean Jeffrey, Sasha McIntyre and Alice Sinkner.

Based on the TV episode *Gee Whiz, Franklin,* written by Simon Racioppa and Richard Elliott.

Kids Can Read is a trademark of Kids Can Press Ltd.

Franklin is a trademark of Kids Can Press Ltd.
The character Franklin was created by Paulette Bourgeois and Brenda Clark.
Text © 2004 Contextx Inc.
Illustrations © 2004 Brenda Clark Illustrator Inc.

Kids Can Press acknowledges the financial support of the Government of Ontario, through the Ontario Media Development Corporation's Ontario Book Initiative; the Ontario Arts Council; the Canada Council for the Arts; and the Government of Canada, through the BPIDP, for our publishing activity.

Published in Canada by
Kids Can Press Ltd.
29 Birch Avenue
Toronto, ON M4V 1E2

Published in the U.S. by
Kids Can Press Ltd.
2250 Military Road
Tonawanda, NY 14150

www.kidscanpress.com

Series editor: Tara Walker
Edited by Jennifer Stokes
Designed by Céleste Gagnon

Printed in Hong Kong, China, by WKT Company Limited

The hardcover edition of this book is smyth sewn casebound.
The paperback edition of this book is limp sewn with a drawn-on cover.

CM 04 0 9 8 7 6 5 4 3 2 1
CM PA 04 0 9 8 7 6 5 4 3 2 1

National Library of Canada Cataloguing in Publication Data

Jennings, Sharon
    Franklin and the contest / Sharon Jennings ; illustrated by Sean Jeffrey, Sasha McIntyre, Alice Sinkner.

(Kids Can read)
The character Franklin was created by Paulette Bourgeois and Brenda Clark.

ISBN 1-55337-491-6 (bound).   ISBN 1-55337-492-4 (pbk.)

I. Jeffrey, Sean II. McIntyre, Sasha III. Sinkner, Alice IV. Bourgeois, Paulette V. Clark, Brenda VI. Title. VII. Series: Kids Can read (Toronto, Ont.)

PS8569.E563F7155 2004   jC813'.54   C2003-904250-2

Kids Can Press is a **Corus** Entertainment company

Franklin and the Contest

Kids Can Press

Franklin can tie his shoes.

Franklin can count by twos.

And Franklin can do lots of
other things, too.

But Franklin cannot do something
for five hours without stopping.

This is a problem.

Franklin wants to win a contest.

One day, Franklin ran home from school.

He grabbed the mail.

There it was!

Gee Whiz Magazine:

The BEST Magazine for Kids!

"YIPPEE!" shouted Franklin.

Franklin sat down to read.

He read about
dinosaurs.

He read about
soccer players.

He read the riddle
page, and he read
the quiz page.

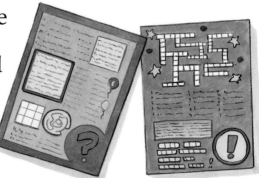

Then Franklin saw the contest page.

"Wow!" said Franklin.

Franklin called his friends.

He ran to meet them at the park.

"*Gee Whiz Magazine* is coming

to Woodland," said Franklin.

He told his friends about the contest.

"Wow!" said everybody.

"We can all enter," said Franklin.

"We have to do something

for five hours without stopping!"

Everybody wanted to enter
the contest.

"I can twiddle my thumbs
for five hours without
stopping," said Beaver.

"I can wiggle my ears,"
said Rabbit.

"I can hum," said Fox.

"I can eat blueberries
and never, *ever* stop!"
said Bear.

Everybody looked at Franklin.

"What can you do?" asked Beaver.

"I will think of something," he said.

Franklin went home to think.

First, he jumped

up and down.

In a minute he was tired.

Then, he stood
on his head.
In half a minute
he fell over.

Next, he rolled
around the yard.

In seconds he was dizzy.
"I will think some more later,"
said Franklin.

For supper, Franklin's mother

gave him fly soup.

"Yummy!" said Franklin.

"I *know* I can eat fly soup for five hours!"

Franklin ate fly soup for one hour.

Then he held his tummy and moaned.

"I will have to think

of something else," he said.

Soon, it was time for bed.

"Think, think, think," said Franklin.

"Why are you frowning?"

asked his mother.

"I'm not frowning," he said.

"I'm thinking."

The next day, and the next day,

and the day after that,

Franklin did lots of things.

He skipped rope.

He spun in a circle.

He mooed

like a cow,

and he clucked

like a chicken.

Franklin could *do* all those things,

but *not* for five hours without stopping.

On Saturday, Franklin woke up early.

"YIPPEE!" he shouted.

"*Gee Whiz Magazine* is coming

to Woodland *today!*"

Then he frowned.

"Think, think, think," he said.

"I need something to do for the contest!"

Franklin walked to the park.

"Think, think, think," he said.

Franklin stood in line to enter the contest.

"Think, think, think," he said.

He met Mr. Possum

from *Gee Whiz Magazine.*

"Why are you frowning?"

asked Mr. Possum.

"I'm not frowning," said Franklin.

"I'm thinking."

"Hey, everybody!" said Mr. Possum.

"Franklin is going to think

for five hours!"

Franklin's friends were surprised.

Franklin was surprised.

"Ready! Set! Go!" shouted Mr. Possum.

Franklin began to think.

27

Franklin kept thinking
when Beaver
stopped twiddling.

He kept thinking
when Rabbit
stopped wiggling.

He kept thinking
when Fox
stopped humming.

And he kept
thinking
when Bear
stopped eating.

"Think, Franklin, think!"

shouted his friends.

"And the winner is … Franklin!"

said Mr. Possum.

"Gee whiz, Franklin!" said his friends.

"You did it! You won!"

"What will you do with your

prize money, Franklin?" asked Bear.

"Hmmm," said Franklin.

"I'll have to think about it!"